THE CHRISTMAS ESCAPE

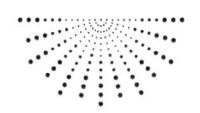

CHAPTER ONE

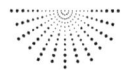

Libby Pearson woke with a smile on her face.

It was a couple of weeks to Christmas and already she could feel magic in the air. She leapt out of bed and hurried into the shower to get ready for work.

She was one of the few people she knew who actually liked getting up to go to the office every day - adored her job and the certain thrill that came with walking into Jefferson & Jacobs Marketing.

Her hair was dark and damp as she slipped her arms into the sleeves of her new red jacket, which matched the pencil skirt she was wearing. Her blouse was white with an oversized collar and cuffs that folded over the ends of the jacket, and she wore black and white polka-dot heels to match her bag.

"Morning Mom and Dad," she said with a smile as

in the living room she passed photos of her parents on the mantle over the fireplace.

Libby always went the long way to the kitchen just to say good morning to them each day. Her parents passed away six years ago. Her father had a heart attack and just one day after he died, her mother went to sleep and didn't wake up.

In the kitchen, the smell of freshly brewed coffee filled her senses and made her feel even happier. She loved coffee in the morning. Food was a second thought, usually something she didn't feel like until lunchtime, but coffee was an absolute must to start the day.

Jingle must've heard her because seconds after she walked into the kitchen, the dog door opened and her friendly, fearless pooch came trotting in. Jingle was a Weimaraner and his stubby tail wagged eagerly at the sight of her.

"Hey boy," she said with a smile as he followed her around the room. "How's it going this morning?"

She poured the coffee into her festive thermal mug, grabbed her lunch from the fridge and packed it into her bag. Libby was trying her best to improve on what she ate, especially so close to the holidays.

She left food for Jingle. He could eat it all and even the bowl too, so she liked to leave a little something extra for him during the day before she gave him his dinner when she got home.

Her parents' house, and forever the Pearson family home was decorated from top to bottom for the season, just like every other house on Clayton Drive.

Nearly every building in the neighbourhood was decorated with hundreds of lights, and those who didn't have hundreds had thousands.

It had taken Libby three days to finish decorating theirs inside and out, but she adored every second of it. Christmas was her favourite time of year and she couldn't imagine it without all the trimmings and festive cheer.

She was barely behind the seat of her little beat-up Fiat 500 when her phone rang. She pressed her Bluetooth button and a second later her brother's voice filled her ears.

"Hey Andy," she greeted as the garage door opened and she began to reverse.

"Sis, don't forget to pick up the turkey," her older brother reminded her. "And you need to make sure to get the cranberries. That canned stuff made Molly itch all night last year."

Her brother's wife was allergic to a great many things, mostly preservatives, so everything had to be made from scratch as Libby had painfully learned last year.

"I remember. I got them up yesterday."

"What about pumpkins? You know how everyone loves your pumpkin and pecan pie," her brother continued.

"I haven't gotten to that yet," she informed him, as she pulled onto the main road and started the journey toward the city. Her office lay at the heart of Rochester's business hub and usually took her about twenty minutes to reach.

"What're you waiting for? You know what the markets will be like the closer to Christmas you get. You risk not getting the good stuff," his brother insisted.

Libby sighed and rolled her eyes. What did Andrew know about markets during the holidays?

In the six years since her parents' passing, Christmas dinner had fallen solely on her shoulders to prepare. She was the one who stood in line at the store to make sure they had all the traditional stuff their mother used to give them.

Though at least her mom had help with the preparations and shopping. Libby had none.

Her phone beeped again and now her sister's name appeared on the screen. "Andy, can you hold? Emma is on the other line."

"OK," her brother replied. "Tell her hi for me and remind her that Kelsey and Brittany are supposed to come over next weekend for their Brownie campout thing."

"I'll remind her," Libby replied before switching the call. "Hi, Ems."

"Libby, did you get the turkey yet?" her sister asked in a rush.

Why was everyone calling her to ask about a dead bird?

"I got it yesterday," she informed her.

"And the cranberries. Andrew was such a mess last year ..."

"Yes, I know. He's actually on the other line and was just telling me the same thing. He also wanted me to remind you about Brit and Kelsey's Brownie camp thing this weekend."

"Right, I almost forgot. Tell him he can drop them at my house for eight. I can give them breakfast before they have to go meet the rest of the troupe."

"Em, why don't you just call and tell him that yourself?" Libby questioned. "You don't need me as an intermediary."

"You're already on the phone with him though," her older sister remarked. "Just tell him what I said OK?"

"Fine." She waited for her sister to continue.

"Well? Aren't you going to tell him?" Emma replied after a moment of silence.

"You meant *now*?" Libby asked incredulously.

"Yes, I want to know what he says."

Libby *really* hated it when her family made her the go-between. Why they didn't just call each other and leave her out of it was beyond her.

She spent the next several minutes playing phone tag with her siblings and listening to them remind Libby of all the things she needed to get done before Christmas.

Story of her life.

CHAPTER TWO

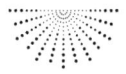

When Libby arrived at the office, the cheer had all but left her.

It was one thing for Andy and Emma to call, but then her other sister Megan plus Emma's twin Eden had also phoned to tell her the same things.

It would be nice if instead of ordering me around, even one *of them would maybe help me for once.*

"Not all, but just one would be *very* much appreciated," she muttered to herself as she got out of the car and walked into the building.

Was it her fault she was the only one who was still single and didn't have a spouse or children? Was it her fault she didn't have in-laws coming for a visit?

She wanted to be married and have a family like the next person, but husbands didn't just drop out of the air like snowflakes nor did children sprout up from cabbage patches.

Libby walked into the office and was greeted by another example of her yuletide efforts. She'd spent all weekend decorating to make sure the staff had something bright and keeping with the season when they arrived on Monday morning.

"Libby, great work - I can't believe you did this all on your own!" Janice the head accountant said as they passed in the hall. "Let me know next time, I'd love to help."

Colleagues were willing to help her when it came to the office, so why wasn't her own family willing to when it came to a family tradition that had been established long before she was even *born*?

They had enjoyed forty-five years of Pearson Christmases in that house; the first five were just her parents before Andrew joined them.

So why was it that she, with only twenty-six years under her belt with their parents and six without, was charged with carrying on the tradition for the entire family? It didn't seem fair, but then again, whoever said life was when it came to family…

Libby loved this time of year but her siblings were taking it too far. They acted as if she had nothing better to do than prepare everything.

Thank goodness for work. If there was one sure thing that could take her mind off of her worries it was that.

As if on cue, the phone rang and her boss's extension appeared on the display.

"Libby, could you come into my office for a few minutes?"

"Sure thing, Steven, I'll be right there."

That was odd. What did he want that she needed to come into his office? Her mind immediately began to conjure up every conceivable scenario to explain it.

Steven Jefferson was a marketing genius and one of the main reasons Libby had applied to the company right out of college.

She walked the long corridor to the door on the right.

"Come in," Steven said and Libby quickly turned the handle and entered.

"Morning," she greeted with a smile as she walked over to one of the chairs facing his desk and took a seat.

He smiled at her. "You did a great job with the office decorating, Libby. I needed to commend you."

He's called her in there to congratulate her on her festive decorating skills? There she was, getting nervous over nothing.

"And since you did such a great job with the office, I thought you would be the perfect person to pitch Hershell Chocolate's new Christmas campaign."

Libby's eyes almost jumped out of her head. Hershell Chocolate was one of their biggest clients.

"What about Amanda?" Libby asked, referring to the executive who usually handled Hershell.

Steven sighed. "Sadly, Amanda has decided to leave us," he informed. "That means we're in need of another senior marketing exec."

Libby's heart began to leap in her chest. Did this mean he was considering *her* for the job?

"I hadn't heard," she replied as she tried to remain calm.

"We were keeping it under wraps until the time came that we could announce her departure and the new appointment," Steven explained. "So we've asked you and Mark Clarke to come up with a presentation. The one Hershell likes best will be who takes over the account and the rest of Amanda's portfolio. Are you up for it?"

"Yes!" Libby answered a little too eagerly.

Steven laughed. "I like your gusto. You have ten days to prepare for the presentation," he continued as he explained what they were looking for in the new plan, and who would be present for the meeting.

This was quite possibly the biggest thing to happen in Libby's career since the day she was hired.

If she landed this account it could make her at the company. Ten days wasn't a lot of time, but she was sure she could make it happen.

"Thank you for considering me," she said as she got to her feet.

"You're a great worker Libby. We notice that here and we reward the effort we see," Steven replied as he got to his feet to show her out. "I look forward to seeing your pitch."

"I won't let you down," she replied determinedly.

CHAPTER THREE

Libby could hardly contain her excitement as she walked back to her office.

She kept looking around to see if anyone was noticing the ridiculously large grin on her face, but they were all busy being productive.

She sat at her desk and stifled a squeal of glee at how the morning had turned around. Then her phone disturbed her joy.

"Hey Megan," she said immediately, recognising the number from the display.

"Libby, can you pick up Justin and Julia from school for me today? Ron's parents are arriving later and his car just broke down on the highway so I have to go get them."

"Meg ..." she tried to interrupt, but her sister's

focus was so honed on her own desires she didn't even hear her.

"They need to be picked up at three and then Justin needs to go to soccer and Julia to dance class."

"Megan, I just got a big project at work. I can't leave the office early today," she protested.

"What? But you're the only person who's close enough to get there on time. What do you want me to do?"

"Maybe call one of their classmate's parents and see if they can?"

"You want to just pass your niece and nephew onto a stranger?" Megan argued.

Libby sighed. Why did they never understand? "Fine. I'll pick them up. I'll just skip lunch and leave early."

"Thanks, sis, you're a gem," her sister replied quickly hanging up.

Libby sighed as she held the dead receiver. "So why don't I feel like one …"

CHAPTER FOUR

Christmas music was playing softly in the background as Libby hummed along.

This truly was the cheeriest time of year, and if all went well, it was going to be even more so for another reason – her promotion.

Her entire career was riding on this one presentation and Libby was determined to nail it.

She'd stayed up late for nights on end trying to come up with a concept when suddenly it struck her while she was watching *A Muppet Christmas Carol* for the millionth time.

"The Hershell people are going to be blown away," she mumbled happily as she worked.

Since then, her design boards were coming along brilliantly. A few more and she'd have everything ready to print and present. She'd called the Henson company regarding the potential use of muppets, and they agreed to discuss a deal if the client came on board.

Everything was working out perfectly; all she had to do was complete and execute it, and the job of new senior marketing executive was all hers.

"Hey Miss Christmas, we were thinking of having a little holiday party on Christmas Eve. What do you say?" her colleague Sharon said as she poked her head around the door to Libby's office.

"I thought we were already having an office party?"

Had something changed and Libby wasn't informed?

"Not here. At my place. Brian and Russel from accounting are down for it. Rob and Joan from printing said they'd join too. And Bobby, Stuart, Leslie and Hailey."

"So I'm the last to know?" Libby mused and Sharon grinned.

"No. I'm just going floor by floor."

"What time?" she asked. Sharon was always looking for a reason to party. She was single, thirty and gorgeous. She had no desire to marry or have a family. She was a career woman with a plan to open her own company in a few years. Libby had no doubt she could do it if only she would get her head out of fun. She spent more time planning events than she did getting her work done.

"Count me in," Libby said with a smile. "I could use some holiday cheer."

Just then her phone rang. It was her sister. Again.

"Hey, Eden."

"Look, I know I said I would pitch in to help you get things ready for Christmas dinner, but I just can't. I am completely swamped. You're going to have to get it done yourself this year, sorry."

"Like every year you mean? Aw, you promised to help this time. It's a lot to do for one person. At least setting up and making dessert would make things easier. I cook the entire meal and clean *and* set up the house…"

"I know, but I really can't. Also, I don't think I'll be able to make dessert either. Adam surprised me with an early Christmas gift and he's taking me to Las Vegas for a few days. We won't be back until Christmas Eve and there's no way after a jaunt like that I'd be able to function."

Libby sighed. There was always a reason more important than helping her.

Eden had one, Andy did … all of her siblings. It was

as if they believed their lives were more important than hers.

Still, Libby did it every year because it wouldn't be Christmas otherwise. A day with no turkey, cranberry sauce, yule log and all the other trimmings just wasn't Christmas.

It was an important time for them as a family.

"I guess I'll have to figure it out on my own again," she sighed.

"Forgive me?"

"Don't I always?" she answered as the weight of the additional preparations she had to make began to weigh on her. She could feel a headache coming on.

"That's because you're great. Love you. See you when I get back."

The call ended and Libby was left wondering how this had happened to her yet again. Sharon was still staring at her when she finally came back to her senses.

"Sorry Sharon, but..."

"But you have stuff to do for Christmas. I know. It's always the same with you. Let me guess, one of your sisters flaked on you again?" her friend said as she entered the room and shut the door.

She crossed the floor to the chair on the opposite side of Libby's desk and sat. Then crossed her legs at the knees and began to strum her perfectly manicured nails on the corner of her desk.

"Why don't you ever just tell them to take a hike and that you're doing something for yourself for a change?" Sharon questioned.

"Because I can't," Libby replied as she picked up some loose papers and moved them from one corner of her desk to the other.

"Why not? You are a thirty-two-year-old puppet. They pull your strings and you do whatever."

"That's not fair," Libby retorted. "It isn't like that."

"Really? What about Thanksgiving?"

Why had she ever told Sharon about that?

It was the day before Thanksgiving. Megan had offered to take on the challenge this year. Everything had been going great until Libby had got a panicked call from her sister telling her how she'd forgotten to defrost the turkey.

She'd burned up the sweet potato mash she'd prepared before time to save her the effort on the day. Everything was going up in flames and she needed Libby's help.

She was always the one to answer the call. She couldn't help it. She was the baby of the family. The one who was always called on to do things whenever her siblings wanted something. It was what she was used to and unfortunately, that hadn't changed in their minds even with the passing of twenty years.

So that day, Libby had left work early. Got into one of the mile-long lines at the butcher shop near her to get a fresh turkey for them to cook. She then went to the market to get the things her sister had wasted before going over to her house to take over the ship.

Megan wasn't used to cooking for so many and she underestimated what it took to prepare for such a big crowd.

Libby also gave up her dinner plans with Todd, the handsome partner from the law firm that occupied the floor below. He'd broken things off with her the day after Thanksgiving. He said she lived her life too much for her family and didn't have time for him.

"I know they're family and you love them, but Libby, there comes a time when you have to tell them 'no,'" Sharon was saying now. "One word. Two letters."

"I know how it's spelt," Libby answered.

"I know you know 'I can't' and 'Maybe next time' but honestly, I don't think I've ever heard you say no - at least not to them. Everything is always 'yes.'"

"I understand what you're saying," Libby sighed. "I just don't know how to do that. How do you disappoint your family at such a special time of year?"

"I don't know. Why don't you ask yours? They do it to you every year."

Sharon's words hurt. Mostly because they were true and Libby knew it.

"Libby, I hate to be the Grinch to your Cindy Lou Hoo, but maybe it's time for you to take a break from all the Christmas is for other people stuff, and look at having a holiday that *you'd* enjoy for a change. Tell me the truth. When the food is gone and it's time to go home, who's the one *also* left with the cleaning up and rearranging the furniture?"

Libby sat back in her seat and thought about it. The more she thought about it, the more unhappy she became.

She couldn't think of a single time since her parents' death that any of her siblings had stayed back after to help either.

"Me," she finally answered.

"Let me guess. They always have children to get to bed, or a long drive, or some other reason why they can't give you a helping hand." Sharon got to her feet and looked at Libby sadly. "I'm sorry to say it hon, but your siblings don't appreciate you. Maybe it's time you look at doing something for yourself. Take a vacation maybe. Go someplace warm or exotic to get away from this cold, and take a break from the crazy shopping lines and big family Christmas dinners. Just my suggestion."

Libby watched as Sharon left. She was gone but the words she'd spoken remained.

She swivelled in her chair and looked out the window at the falling snow outside.

A vacation from Christmas? It sounded lovely. More than lovely, it sounded like a dream, but there was no way she could do it.

Christmas was about family and togetherness. Libby couldn't just up and leave hers.

Could she?

CHAPTER FIVE

The phone rang agains as she sat thinking.

She hesitated to answer it when she saw that it was Megan on the line again. Still, she just couldn't resist picking up.

Hi Libs. It's me. I need a favor."

"What is it? I'm pretty busy here."

"Nothing too urgent. I just need you to pick up some groceries for me at the market. My in-laws are here as you know and I didn't get to the store yet. They won't have anything for dinner."

"Why can't you pick something up on your way home?"

"You know Laurel doesn't eat takeout. Besides, I have to work late tonight. By the time I get in it will be very late."

"And what about Ron? They're his parents," Libby pointed out.

"He was called out of town unexpectedly. It's just me and them at home for the next two days. You know how Laurel and I are. She tries everything she can think of to find fault. She's upset that I haven't made her a grandmother yet. You know what she says. …"

"'A woman isn't a woman unless she has children.' Yes, I remember," Libby groaned. She knew what was coming. She was going to have to skip lunch and leave early again to help her sister.

"Libs, please?"

"Alright, alright," she conceded huffily.

"Excellent! Thank you. Oh, could you possibly pick up my dry cleaning from too? It's on your way. And if you could make something quick for dinner I'd be eternally grateful. If Laurel has to cook there'll be no end of complaining…."

Libby was speechless. Her sister had gone from her collecting groceries to picking up laundry and cooking for in-laws that weren't even her own!

"Megan, I'm working on a really big project right now. I'm up for a promotion."

"That's great. I'm sure you'll get it."

"But I really need to work on my presentation."

"You can still do that when you get home can't you? How long do you have?

"Just a few days."

"See, plenty of time to complete the task successfully. But today I really need you. Please, little sister?"

Libby sighed. She couldn't very well leave Megan in a bind. Her mother-in-law was the she-beast from hell.

If she didn't help now, she'd hear about it forever when Megan called to complain about the torment she was under.

"I'll leave work early, but you owe me," Libby replied tersely.

"I will treat you to dinner. Order anything you like."

"You owe me five dinners already."

"And you'll get them. As soon as I can, you'll get them." There was a pause. "Libs, I really have to go now. Do you have everything? Groceries, dry-cleaning, and dinner for my in-laws?"

"I have it, Megan."

"Great. Call you later."

The phone hung up immediately and Libby set the receiver down with a sigh. "No, you won't."

. . .

SHE GOT HOME AROUND NINE. The grocery store lines were longer than expected and it took a while to get to Megan's. Once there, she prepared the meal and chatted with her sister's in-laws. She'd stayed as long as she could to be polite, but Megan had yet to arrive by the time she left.

Libby strolled into the house and was met by a delighted Jingle. "Hey boy."

The little dog barked and began to circle, sniffing for any hidden treats.

"I didn't bring you anything, sorry. You're smelling the dinner I made for Megan," she said to him as she shuffled to the kitchen, kicking her heels off in the living room and walking barefoot.

When she passed the phone in the living room she was shocked to find there was a message. She pressed the button.

"Libs, you forgot the shirt I wanted to wear tomorrow –"

She stopped the message midway. Well, at least Megan had been honest.

She *did* call her later.

CHAPTER SIX

The next day Libby found herself sitting on the couch in her living room looking over old photos.

Their father had been a constant photographer since before any of them were born. He had every traditional photo one could take during the holidays.

There were some of their mother putting the turkey in the oven. Some of Megan and Andy as children fighting over the last piece of stuffing. There was even a baby picture of Libby with fat cheeks and her face covered in chocolate frosting from the Yule log.

"Such good times …" she said with a sad smile. She missed her parents. There were hardly any holiday photos since they had left them.

Libby had tried to step into her father's shoes but it was impossible when she was doing everything else.

Still, she managed to take a few shots from time to time.

One year she had enlisted her eight-year-old nephew to do pictures and he'd taken plenty but there were far more out of focus than in.

Then she found a picture of her mother surrounded by all of her children. They were all grinning and her mom's cheeks were rosy and her smile bright.

"I miss you, Mom," Libby said softly. "This time of year just isn't the same without you and Dad. Things have changed and I don't know if you'd be happy about it. Andy and the others are hardly here anymore. It's almost Christmas and here I am again doing everything on my own. When you were around this would never have happened."

She chuckled lightly. "Do you remember? You and I would team up and tackle every task. The others would come to help once the smell of the food started to fill the house." She laughed sadly. "There's no one here now to do that though. I buy the groceries. Clean and decorate the house. Cook the food and clean it up after."

The phone rang. It always rang more often during the holidays.

"Hey big bro," Libby greeted, as she slid down on

the couch and put her feet up on the arm of it.

Andy sounded as if he was driving. She could hear the sound of the traffic blowing past the window and the sound of horns honking.

"I need to borrow your laptop if I could."

"What's the matter with yours?"

"It died this morning and I need it to finish a document for work tomorrow. Can I borrow yours?"

"OK, but you'll have it drop it back to me straight after. I need it for an important presentation that's in two days."

"I'll have it back. No worries."

"I mean it, Andy. I need it back tomorrow so that I can finish the project on time. It might land me a promotion."

"It's about time you got one. You're the best they have."

"Thanks. It's for the Hershell Chocolate account."

"Hershell? That's a big deal. Are you sure you're ready?"

Her eyes widened. Didn't he just say she was the best they had? Libby did her best not to express her disappointment.

"Where are you?" she asked him.

"On my way to you."

"You mean you already knew that I'd let you borrow it?" she asked, a little taken aback.

"Sorry. But you never let us down, sis. It's something we can always be sure of."

CHAPTER SEVEN

"Andy, it's me again. Why haven't you called me back? I need the laptop. Call me back."

Since she'd leant him the laptop Libby couldn't reach Andy on the phone.

She paced her office again, as nettles covered her skin.

The client would be here today and her stupid brother had done a disappearing act. Which she wouldn't have minded if it weren't for the fact that he still had her laptop!

Her phone rang minutes later and a wave of relief washed over her as she saw her brother's name appear on screen.

"Andy, where on earth are you? I've been calling and calling."

"I had to fly out to New York."

"*What?* New York, New York? But what about my laptop? I told you I needed it."

"I'm sorry. I had to take it with me, but I'm back now and I have it."

Libby's heart dropped into her stomach. "Oh my God. Where are you now?"

"At the airport. I just landed. I'm headed to you as soon as I get through arrivals."

Libby ran her fingers through her hair in dismay.

"The *airport*? Andy, that's too far. You won't get here in time. I told you I needed it back before the presentation!"

"I'm sorry. The work thing totally slipped my mind."

"The biggest day of my life and it slipped your mind?" Libby cried in disbelief.

She hung up. Her phone rang several times afterward but she wouldn't look at it.

Everything was ruined. Her PowerPoint was on that laptop and there was no way for her to access it otherwise. "I should have saved what I had to a memory stick ... why didn't I do that?" she winced, as tears filled her eyes.

The client would be arriving soon and she had nothing to show them.

Now, Libby walked toward Steven's office. She had to tell him the bad news. She had no idea how her boss would take it, but she was disappointed enough for both of them.

She passed Mark Clarke in the hall on the way there. There would be no end to his arrogance once he got the promotion. The entire marketing team would live to regret her foolishness.

Libby's pace slowed as she approached Steven's office. She looked at his nameplate outside, written in gold and trembled.

She couldn't believe this was happening. Her boss had given her a chance and now she was here to beg for another.

She took a deep breath, raised her hand and knocked.

"Come in."

Steven greeted her with a smile that Libby tried to return but failed.

Just as she'd failed at the task he'd given her.

"Libby, all ready for later?" he asked with a smile.

She hesitated. "Actually no. There was a problem with my laptop and I don't have the PowerPoint file to hand."

The words left her lips like molasses from a bottle on a cold day.

Steven's gaze levelled at her.

"What do you mean? Can't you just upload it to a PC here?"

She shook her head. She swallowed the lump in her throat.

"I didn't save and download it because it wasn't quite finished. Tomorrow - I can have it completed tomorrow. Is there any chance the client might be persuaded to delay until then?"

Libby was internally crossing her fingers and her toes.

She just needed another chance. She could have everything ready by tomorrow. She just needed time.

"There is nothing I can do for you, Libby. The client's only free window was today. Plus the board wants to make the announcement as soon as possible regarding the new senior marketing executive." Steven stood and walked toward her. He laid a comforting hand on her arm. "I'm sorry."

That was it. One mistake and she'd lost the biggest opportunity of her life.

She should never have allowed her brother to borrow her laptop. It was the company's, so she really should've known better anyway, but he needed her help.

Now she was paying for it.

"Steven," she pleaded. "Isn't there any way? I know this is really good."

"I'm sorry Libby. This was a one-time chance."

She stood dumbfounded as Steven turned his back on her and walked back to his seat. He sat with both hands on the armrests and looked at her. "If Mark successfully completes the presentation, I will announce his appointment at the Christmas party."

Libby stared at him for several seconds as she tried to internalize what he'd said.

She'd blown it. It was over. Really and truly over.

"Thank you for the opportunity. I'm so sorry I let you down," Libby said softly as she lowered her eyes in shame.

"Not more than me. I was sure you were the best person for this position, but I had to prove it to the board," Steven said bitterly. "It'll be a hard pill to swallow when I have to go back to them."

"Steven, just twenty-four hours?" Libby pleaded again. "That's all I need. I know my presentation will blow them away. I'm sure of it. If you could just post-pone it for a day? A few hours, even. I can get it all together for you. I can make this happen."

"I wish I could, Libby. I really wish I could. But there is nothing I can do. Hershells set the timing because it worked with their schedule. There is no tomorrow or a few hours. It's now or never."

CHAPTER EIGHT

Libby could barely process anything as she trudged slowly back to her office.

People passed her on the way to wish her good luck with the presentation, but nothing reached her.

She returned to her office, closed and locked the door and then sat at her desk and wept.

Her eyes were puffy and sore by the time someone knocking on her door got her attention.

She forced herself to wipe her face and got a tissue to blow her nose before she dared open it.

Unlocking the door, she took a deep breath. Sharon was standing there with the saddest look on her face.

"I heard."

Libby let her in and then quickly closed the door

behind her. People in the hall were staring. She couldn't deal with them right now.

"What happened?" her friend asked.

Libby walked around her desk and flopped into her chair.

"You had this. What went wrong?" Sharon persisted.

"Me. That's what went wrong. Me."

"You? What did you do?"

"I loaned my brother the laptop when he had an emergency with work. I told him I needed it back the next day. He forgot and took it with him to New York."

Sharon's eyes looked as if they were about to explode from her skull. "Are … you … *kidding* me?" she bellowed

"Shhh…keep your voice down."

"How can *you* keep your voice down? Your brother shafts you over the biggest opportunity of your life, and you're this calm about it?"

"It was my fault. I should never have lent it to him in the first place. It was company property, not mine. I was the idiot here."

"Libby, are you for real? You're blaming yourself for this? Your brother is the absolute worst! Yes, you were wrong to give him the laptop, but he was worse for not bringing it back when he knew you needed it. He really took it to New York?" Sharon's head was shaking as she sighed deeply.

"It doesn't matter now," Libby stated. "It's over."

"Libby, for goodness sake, get angry. Do something. This can't go on. You can't spend the rest of your life being your siblings' scapegoat for everything. You need to think of having a life of your own. I know you want to hold on to traditions, but for your own sake, you need to create new ones."

Sharon was on her feet a moment later and striding to the door. "Think about it. Someone has to give."

Leaving Libby alone and confused.

She thought about everything that had happened over the last few days and weeks - the endless demands and requests for 'favours'.

And Andy's words as he casually drove to borrow the laptop he already knew she'd lend him.

You never let us down, sis. It's something we can always be sure of.

CHAPTER NINE

The following afternoon, Libby dropped her stuff at her front door, stomped into the living room and flopped down on the couch with a groan.

Andrew had since apologised about the incident with the laptop by saying there would be other promotions and not to sweat the small stuff. Small stuff. He saw the biggest opportunity of her career as 'small stuff.'!

It was getting beyond ridiculous.

Today she'd received another call from Eden informing her that *her* in-laws had come in early to surprise them, and could Libby take her children and their friends Christmas shopping?

She'd spent three hours with eight children between the ages of six and ten, as she tried to help them manage their money and pick up the toys they were searching for.

It was a test of anyone's nerves and Libby's were well and truly fried.

Jingle trotted into the room and flopped on the rug by her feet. "Hey little guy," she said with a frustrated sigh. He looked at her with his big dark eyes and snorted. "That's exactly how I feel," she replied as she stretched out a hand to scratch behind his ears.

She lay on the couch for several minutes as she decided whether she wanted to move or not. Her feet hurt, her back hurt and she was hungry. She had taken the children shopping but she wasn't about to manage all of them at one table with food too.

She rolled onto her side and noticed the light blinking on the phone. Another message from Andy. Maybe he'd had second thoughts and was calling to properly apologise?

"Hi, Libs. Meet me at the mall tomorrow? I need some help finding a present for Molly. I'll be there around five. Meet you at the west entrance. Bye!"

She couldn't speak. Tears were stinging the backs of her eyes.

"He didn't even ask," she said to herself as a tear rolled down her cheek. *None* of them ever asked, or if they did, they took it for granted that the answer would be yes and if it wasn't they made a fuss until it was.

"OK, that's *it*," she announced, so loud that it made Jingle jump up from his nap. The dog gave a started yelp as he tried to figure out what was going on. "Enough."

She got to her feet and hurried upstairs, Jingle scurrying after her.

"Someplace warm," she muttered to herself as she began rummaging in her closet. She pulled out her suitcase and tossed it on the bed.

Libby wasn't thinking, she was just packing. She found her bathing suit, some shorts, a few dresses, and shoes. Anything that would work.

"If they think I'm sticking around to be their Christmas Girl Friday this year, they're mistaken," she said angrily. Jingle was completely bewildered and stuck his nose in her stuff to see what was going on.

When the suitcase was packed she opened her laptop and began searching for flights. Her favorite discount site had tons of offers but nothing was grabbing her.

That is until she saw a special and her eyes widened. *Hawaii?*

Perfect.

Libby didn't hesitate; she booked the flight and

used her discount coupon to get a further $25 off her ticket.

"Now where to stay..." she asked as she began another search. Jingle barked beside her. "I know. You're hungry," she commented as her fingers nimbly skated over the keys. Her eyes flicked through pictures of potential accommodation, but it was taking longer than expected and Jingle was getting increasingly agitated.

While Libby was starting to feel increasingly better, as the prospect of a quieter, more relaxing Christmas materialized.

She hummed a festive tune as she danced around the kitchen pulling together something for herself for dinner. She grabbed kibble from the cupboard and a can of canned dog food. She mixed them together and put them in Jingle's bowl. He was already eating before she got it to the floor, and so she returned to her laptop.

There were so many options to choose from, but she didn't want to stay anywhere too commercial or crazy.

So the Marriott and the like were definitely out.

Then Libby came across an option for a guesthouse just a few minute's drive from the airport, and right on the beach.

"Kalea Inn," she mused out loud, as she began to skim the reviews. They were all overwhelmingly positive. The place rated four and a half stars which was excellent, and the price was perfect.

Finally, her decision was made. She pressed the 'Book' button and it was done.

Libby smiled to herself as she leaned against the kitchen counter.

This year, she was getting out of town and heading for somewhere a million miles from small-town Christmas Central.

She needed an escape.

CHAPTER TEN

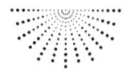

Four days later Libby was standing outside Kona Airport waiting for her ride.

The guesthouse owner had sent her an email about her booking at the Kalea Inn later that same night and they'd been corresponding over the past few days to ensure that everything was ready for her arrival.

The second she stepped off the plane Libby found herself with a beautiful purple lei around her neck and she smiled.

Outside, the sun was blissfully bright and warm, and the air tropical. It was just what she was hoping for.

A warm breeze blew across her face as she waited for someone from the inn to pick her up. She got her phone out and called home.

"Hey Sharon how's Jingle?"

Her friend was dog-sitting for the week she'd be gone.

Before leaving she'd called Andy to let him and the others know she was going away and wasn't going to be back until after Christmas.

That didn't go over well but Libby hadn't listened long enough to hear his surprise or remonstration.

She'd made up her mind and she wasn't letting anyone change it.

A jeep pulled up and a man got out.

The vehicle was like something she'd seen on safari videos on Discovery Channel, but the side of it read Kalea Inn.

Libby's eyes grew large at the sight of the man walking toward her. He was over six feet tall and the roots of his hair were dark but the ends were lighter from the sun.

His skin was golden tan and his short-sleeved cotton shirt clung to his muscles. On his left arm, the ends of a black tattoo peeked out from beneath the sleeve. His chin was covered in a short, neatly cropped beard beneath a moustache.

The guy should be on the cover of a romance novel.

The man strode toward her, a folded sign in his hands which he opened as he looked around.

It took Libby a few seconds to notice the name on the card was her own.

She walked toward him and dragged her bag behind her.

"I'm Libby," she said brightly as she flashed him a smile. He looked at her and gave a polite smile so quick that if she blinked she would've missed it.

"Rob," he nodded. "Welcome to Kohala."

"Thanks. Nice to meet you. It's good to have a face to go with the name," she replied amiably. She was smiling more than she should but she couldn't help it. She was in a tropical paradise for the holidays, and her driver looked like someone from a movie.

"Sure," he replied as he took Libby's luggage and started for the jeep.

She looked around as she followed him. "Isn't there anyone else?"

"You're it today," Rob said as he hoisted her bag into the back. "You can sit up front with me," he added as he walked to the driver's side and got in.

Libby walked around the front of the vehicle. He opened the door for her from the inside and she climbed in.

The cabin of the car was neat. She couldn't help the surreptitious inspection as she got in. His car was much cleaner than hers. She always had an extra pair of shoes or three on the passenger side.

Rob started the engine and they began the journey to the inn. Lava fields spread before her in red and black earth splendor, amidst verdant palm trees.

Libby could hardly believe she was really in Hawaii.

"It's so beautiful," she commented to herself as she stared out at the landscape.

"You said it was your first time on the island?" Rob questioned. He was driving with one hand and leaning on the window with the other.

"Very first," Libby answered. "And you? You've been here long?"

"Seven years," he answered shortly.

"I guess this beauty is normal to you, then."

Rob didn't answer. He just looked out the window.

"So how far is it?" she asked eventually.

"Just over twenty minutes. The inn is just up past Waialea Beach."

Libby smiled at the way the strange names rolled off his tongue. He looked like he belonged in an ad for lumberjacks or something. She could definitely see him in one of her ad campaigns. He'd be perfect.

"What?" he asked shortly. She was so lost in her own head she hadn't realized she was staring.

"Sorry," she laughed. "I was just thinking."

"Your mother never taught you that you don't stare?"

Now Libby was a bit taken back by his abruptness. "Actually she did. Sorry," she replied shortly.

So much for an Aloha welcome.

THE DRIVE TOOK LESS time than she imagined. Twenty minutes went by very quickly when everything around was so spectacular.

The next thing Libby knew they were stopped outside a simple two-storey building, painted in cream with a brown roof and trim.

What stood out to her was that there wasn't a single Christmas decoration apparent. She glanced around a little more while Rob unloaded her bag.

Nope, nothing.

"You guys don't decorate for the holidays?" she asked in surprise. The rest of the Big Island she'd seen on the way had some signs of festive cheer, but not the Kalea Inn.

"I don't do Christmas," Rob answered gruffly. "This way to check in."

Libby's forehead wrinkled as she followed him into the building.

What did he mean that he didn't *do* Christmas? Who didn't do Christmas?

But there wasn't a smile on his face and she knew instinctively that he wasn't joking.

They were met at reception by a pretty dark-haired woman who had a brilliant smile.

"Apikalia, could you see that Ms Pearson gets checked in? She's in room nine," Rob informed her as he left Libby's bag at the desk and then disappeared into a room behind it.

"Mele Kalikimaka," the receptionist said brightly. "Welcome to the Kalea Inn."

Libby swallowed, realising that if she truly wanted to escape Christmas, she'd very definitely picked the right place.

CHAPTER ELEVEN

The next couple of days passed by in a blur and Libby was loving every second of it. She'd *definitely* made the right choice to embark on a last minute adventure.

Her room was on the top floor overlooking the ocean. The guesthouse had its own private beach, a secluded cove up the coast from Waialea.

In fact, there was nothing else nearby as far as the eye could see; the absolute perfect getaway.

It was also nice to have people taking care of her instead of the other way round. Libby usually didn't mind, but after a while, it began to weigh on you, especially when the people you were doing it for didn't seem to care just how much it was taking out of you.

Today she wore a red sundress with a white tropical flower print along the skirt. It was sleeveless and showed off her slightly toned arms.

She'd worked very hard for that little bit of tone. Libby tended to be softer; she wasn't overweight, but she had gentle curves and a propensity to gain even more of those if she didn't pay attention.

Mint green sandals were on her feet. She had a matching bag too, but she didn't have plans to leave the inn that day. She just wanted to spend it on the beach enjoying the warm breezes and golden sunshine.

She walked down to the breakfast area and found it relatively full, but there were still a few tables available.

The inn had twelve rooms and they were all occupied for the festive season.

Libby had briefly encountered several of her fellow guests over the past few days, but none touched her heart like Naomi - a seventy-three-year-old woman who reminded her so much of her mother.

Now she walked over to where the older woman was sitting. "Good morning."

"Nice to see you, dear. Join me?"

Libby didn't need to be asked twice. She pulled out the chair beside Naomi and took a seat. "Thanks for letting me sit with you. How're you doing today?"

"I'm very well thank you. How are you?"

"Great. Have you ordered already?" She skimmed over the menu. There weren't many choices, but what they had was fresh and always wonderful.

"I was just waiting for the waitress," Naomi informed her. "What are your plans today?"

"Nothing," Libby sighed happily. "Just enjoying the sunshine. What about you?" she asked as the waitress poured water when they'd placed their orders.

"Well, I'm on a mission today actually," the older woman said intriguingly. She then turned to the vacant seat beside her and picked up a silver urn.

"I'm going to see my Charlie off," she added with a gentle smile.

"Oh Naomi …" Libby began but she wasn't sure what she wanted to say.

The older woman had mentioned her husband had died but she didn't realize it was so recently.

Naomi smiled as she patted the top of the urn lovingly. "He always wanted to come back here," she said. "He proposed to me on this island fifty years ago. We planned to come back this Christmas to commemorate it, but poor Charlie didn't make it."

Libby swallowed the lump that had formed in her throat. She couldn't help it, hearing Naomi's heart-breaking words made her want to cry.

"Don't get upset," the other woman said brightly. "Charlie wouldn't want anyone crying over him. He always lived his life a second at a time, and he enjoyed every minute of it. That's why I'm here. He wanted me to come, even though he wasn't going to be with me in body, but promised he'd be with me in spirit." Naomi hugged the urn to her before setting it back on its seat.

"Where on the island are you going?" Libby asked as the waitress returned with their coffee and juice.

"To Pu'u Ku'ili," she replied, referring to the famed old cinder cone, a popular sightseeing spot on the island.

"How are you getting there?"

"I've arranged a ride," the woman answered.

Libby looked aghast. "You're going to do this alone?"

"It's fine. I promised Charlie. The sooner the better to get it over with."

Libby was resolute. There was no way she was going to allow that. "If you don't mind the company … may I come with you?"

A small smile spread across Naomi's face. "Are you sure?"

"I'd love it if you'd allow me," Libby replied. "I'd feel a whole lot better knowing you weren't alone."

"I'd like that."

The pair continued to sit and talk while they waited for breakfast to arrive. Once it did they took turns sampling from the other's choice and laughing about having made the wrong decision for themselves.

It felt good to just enjoy a meal with someone and make plans with them, instead of hearing their demands.

Libby truly wanted to be there for Naomi. She couldn't imagine saying goodbye forever to the one you loved would be easy.

She'd never been married, not even close, but she remembered the interactions of her parents. Theirs was the ideal that she based all her relationships on.

Her parents had a love that transcended most norms. They genuinely loved one another and sacrificed for the other.

It seemed Naomi and Charlie's marriage had been the same.

CHAPTER TWELVE

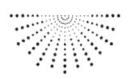

After breakfast, Libby excused herself momentarily to get her bag from her room and rushed back, unwilling to keep Naomi waiting long.

On the way, she ran into Rob – literally. Their shoulders collided as she was going up the stairs and he was coming down.

"Sorry," she apologized in a rush as she continued on her journey up. She felt his questioning gaze follow her but she didn't turn around.

Minutes later she was rushing through the reception area outside to where she'd told Naomi she'd meet her.

The older woman was already standing beside the inn's jeep.

"All set?" Libby asked.

"We were waiting for you," Naomi replied.

"We?"

A second later Rob stepped out from the other side of the jeep. He looked at her silently and Libby felt the hairs on the back of her neck stand on end.

He had an intense expression on his face that even though not unpleasant, formed knots in her stomach.

"Rob said he'd take us," Naomi informed her.

"Let's get you ladies boarded so we can get going," he stated as he stepped forward to help Naomi into the jeep. He turned to Libby after and gave her a hand into the back.

She sat on the bench that lined the back of the jeep's flatbed and watched as the lava fields once again came into view.

Once or twice she thought she caught Rob's eyes looking back at her in the rearview mirror. It was nice of him to offer to take Naomi here today.

And a little perplexing how he could be so cold one minute, then do something kind and courteous the next.

It wasn't long before they arrived at Pu'u Ku'ili.

Rob drove them as far as he could along the trail, but they still had to walk a short distance to get to the top.

He held Naomi's hand while Libby carried the urn.

When they reached the summit Libby stood on the cone and looked around her.

The view was unforgettable. Inland, the earth was charred and the dirt was either black or dark red. There was hardly any vegetation nearby, but in the distance, she could see sprigs of grass and the green of a few shrubs.

Towards the ocean, she could see buildings standing uniformly together, their roofs various shades of brown and more greenery to be found nearby. The ocean was the most beautiful blue she'd ever seen. Paler near the shore, it deepened from azure to a rich cerulean.

It was breathtaking.

"Give Charlie to me," Naomi asked then, as Libby stood staring. She nodded quickly and handed the urn over.

Then she stepped back a little to where Rob stood a few feet away, to allow Naomi the privacy needed for her last farewell to her husband.

Libby watched as it unfolded. She wanted to make sure Naomi was all right, but she also couldn't help but admire how unaffected and unflinching she was to do something she herself was sure would have her in tears.

She wondered where the woman got the strength

from.

"It must be such a horrible thing to lose the one you love," she mumbled to Rob as they watched. "To have to say goodbye after so many wonderful years together. Knowing that you will never see them again."

He exhaled. "Hurts no matter how long you were together," he muttered, much to her surprise.

Libby turned to face him but found he wasn't looking at her at all but at Naomi.

Her gaze shifted to where the older woman stood. Was that it? The reason he always seemed so cagey and distant? Had he lost someone too?

She turned back to Rob and this time their eyes met. "Why did you come?" he asked. "You don't even know her."

"You don't have to know someone well to want to be there for them through something difficult," she answered, then turned back to Naomi. "I just didn't want to let her do this alone."

"Neither did I," he said and Libby's eyes moved back to him. "Like you said, it isn't something you should do alone, especially at her age."

Maybe he wasn't as boorish as she'd first believed him to be. Maybe he was just a man who was dealing with something she could never understand. Something that Naomi could though.

Did Rob truly identify with the older woman's loss? Was that why he couldn't let her say goodbye alone?

Libby had more questions now than when she'd first met him. Who exactly was Rob and why was he in Kohala?

He obviously wasn't a native Hawaiian. So what had brought him to the islands to run the inn?

The faint sound of a song wafted toward Libby's ears and both she and Rob again focused their attention back on Naomi. She was singing.

It was an old song, something from the forties or fifties Libby guessed. She was swaying in place as she turned the urn over and allowed her late husband's ashes to spill into the breeze to every note.

"Goodbye Charlie ..." Libby whispered to herself as she watched the scene.

Now the older woman walked toward them, the empty urn hugged to her chest. She smiled. "He's gone now," she said. "He'd be happy."

Libby couldn't help it; she had to give Naomi a hug. The older woman accepted her embrace and patted her back soothingly. "Thank you for being here - both of you," she said.

"You're welcome," Rob answered quietly. "It was an honour."

CHAPTER THIRTEEN

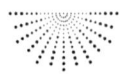

Later, Libby couldn't sleep, still affected by the events of the day. She kept thinking of her family and wondering how they were doing.

Her siblings had been calling her incessantly since her arrival, and while she was happy to send the odd text, she still refused to take any calls.

This trip was all about escape, some time for herself, away from them.

She stood on the balcony outside her room and looked out over the dark water. The sky and sea seemed to meet like ink on the horizon. Only the stars differentiated one from the other.

She leaned against the rail, the silk nightgown she wore danced around her calves as she watched the white peaks of waves appear and disappear in the distance.

Half an hour passed and she was still unable to sleep. So she changed into a sundress and went downstairs for a walk.

Voices coming from the dining room caught her attention as she headed for the front door.

She followed the sound to find Rob and two other men sitting talking around a small table.

"Seems we aren't the only night owls," the first man commented when he saw her in the doorway. She recognised him as another guest.

He was cleanly shaven with a bald head and a slender face.

"I'm sorry. I didn't mean to intrude. I just heard voices ..." Libby explained hesitantly.

"No intrusion. Come on in," the man said with a friendly wave of his hand beckoning her to join them.

Another man sat beside him. He looked similar, though his hair was dark and closely cropped, and his face fuller and more tanned.

"I'm Nate," the other guest said as he extended her hand to her. "This is my twin brother Greg."

Now Libby saw the resemblance. It was in the eyes. They both had bright blue eyes.

"Libby," she answered as she shook each man's hand in turn. She looked at their host. "Rob."

He nodded but said nothing. He was reclined in his seat with his foot folded over the other casually and his arms crossed over his stomach.

"So what brings you to the island?" Greg asked with a smile.

She smiled. "Escaping Christmas," she admitted truthfully. "Family mostly."

"They giving you a hard time?"

"More like they don't see me as anything more than their go-fetch-it girl," she chuckled but there was no mirth to it. "My favourite time of the year, and all I hear from them is what they need from me. No one ever seems to realize that I need things too."

"Material stuff you mean?" Nate questioned.

"No. More for them to be there for me the way I'm always there for them. It gets pretty tiring being the one whom everyone depends on, yet there is no one there when you need the same."

"Well, my poor brother knows all about that," Nate laughed and Libby looked at him and Greg curiously. "I have cancer," he blurted out then and she was taken completely by surprise.

She fumbled for something to say and found herself tongue-tied.

"You don't have to say anything. You were on the subject of dependency and I just wanted to make things clear from the start," Nate continued.

"I'm so sorry," she muttered.

"I told you that you didn't have to say anything," he smiled. "People always say they're sorry. It's nice but unnecessary. I'm alright. I've made peace with everything."

"So Kohala is part of your adventure?" Libby asked.

"It's the seventh thing on my bucket list."

Libby was completely astounded at Nate's positivity. She had never met anyone who knew they were dying.

She couldn't imagine what that must feel like to know that your end was imminent. The thought gave her a slight chill.

"Rob was telling us that you helped Naomi scatter her husband's ashes the other day," Nate continued while his brother sat quietly and Libby could immediately see that while he had accepted his fate, Greg had not.

They chatted on for a while before eventually, Nate yawned. "I think it's time for me to go. I'm getting tired."

"Goodnight guys," Greg said as he helped his brother to his feet.

"Goodnight to you both," Libby replied. "See you guys in the morning."

"Maybe we can do breakfast?" Nate suggested. "I'd love to hear more about your work for the chocolate company."

"See you here."

Libby watched the brothers as they went.

It was odd, but meeting them only made her think of her own family even more. Nate and Greg depended on each other and there was no animosity between them. One was dying and the other was doing everything he could to be there for him.

It made her feel like her problems with her siblings were silly really.

Now, she turned to look at Rob. He'd remained quiet for most of the conversation, only choosing to say something if a question was directed to him.

She shifted uncomfortably in her seat. Maybe she should go now too? It wasn't as if Rob was going to stay on and chat. He hardly ever spoke to her.

"How's Naomi?" he asked then.

"Great. I had dinner with her earlier."

"Good," Rob replied. "The other day must've brought up a lot of memories. Good and bad."

Libby watched him carefully. The visit to Pu'u Ku'ili had affected more than just Naomi.

"Who did you lose?" she asked softly. She watched him as she spoke and his face was impassive as he turned to her.

"What makes you think I lost someone?"

She smiled weakly. "I recognize it. When I lost my parents I looked like that whenever someone started talking about them," Libby explained.

Rob stared at her for a long time and she could see the hesitation in his eyes. "My wife."

"Your wife? I'm ... so sorry."

"Her name was Kalea. I named this place after her. She was born on the island and wanted to come back to start a business and give back to the community. We poured everything we had into getting this place. Then she died, so I was left to run it alone."

Libby couldn't imagine how he felt losing his wife. "I truly am sorry Rob. May I ask what happened to her?"

"A brain tumour. We were married for just over a year when it got her," he continued. "On Christmas Eve."

Which explained why there were no decorations and why Rob didn't do Christmas. He was still missing his wife.

"She loved this time of year. It was what she lived for really. The holidays and decorations, and family get-togethers. Kalea always wanted to make people happy."

Libby felt a tear roll down her cheek as Rob talked about his late wife. There was still so much love in his voice.

"I'm sorry. This is hard for you. I shouldn't have asked," Libby apologised as she wiped her cheek.

"I don't know why I'm telling you actually," he continued. "I never talk about her to anyone. It must be everything with Naomi ... and now Nate that has me thinking about her." He turned to her. "Sorry for getting you down."

"Don't apologize. I asked."

"When did you lose your parents?" He had turned in his seat to face her better. It was the first time Libby noticed how bright his eyes were, even in sadness.

"Six years ago. They died days apart, and it was pretty much left to me to take over everything they cared about," she admitted. "All our family's stuff. The house. Traditions. It all became my responsibility."

"Why you? Didn't you say you had siblings?"

"Four of them," Libby answered. "They all have families of their own. Children and in-laws. They don't have much time for anything else."

"Including you, I take it?"

Her cheeks warmed at the inquiry. "Sometimes I

feel like I'm a servant instead of their sister. Running around to pick up their children. Collect their dry-cleaning and deal with upholding our family stuff all on my own. It's been hard. Honestly, this year I was so tired of having to do everything for the holidays that I decided that I wasn't - going to do it, I mean. That's why I came here."

"Do you hate them?"

Her eyes grew wide. "No. Of course not. I love them a lot. That's why it hurts so much to be treated like I don't matter to them. That what's important to me, means nothing to them at all."

"I understand," Rob said as he got to his feet. "It isn't easy to bear the weight of a legacy on your shoulders. Or someone else dream."

Libby stood too, feeling tired all of a sudden, and realising that she and Rob kind of understood each other in some strange way.

He was doing all of this in the name of a wife who could no longer fulfil her dream, while she was doing all she could to keep her parent's traditions alive.

"Walk you back to your room?" he stated as he started for the door.

"How do you do it?" she asked, following as he left the dining room and up the stairs.

"Do what?"

"Continue on every day on your own with no one here who understands?"

"I surf," Rob said with a smile. "When I'm out on the waves there isn't anything for me to worry about. It's just me and the waves. It makes me think of her. She loved the water. We met at a surfing competition in California. It was love on the waves," he said with a smile. "I knew the first time I saw her cruise through that curl that I'd found the perfect woman for me."

Libby smiled. "It sounds wonderful."

"It was wonderful." He looked around him. "I know she would've done more with this place, especially now, but I just can't seem to get my mind there."

"I'll be honest with you. I was wondering about it when I arrived. I was surprised that there were no Christmas decorations, or anything remotely festive."

He sighed. "I don't know why I should bother really. No one's complaining. Except for you," he added lightly.

Libby considered what he'd said as they walked the corridor to her room.

There were quite a few people here escaping the holidays for their own, mostly sad reasons. Even the owner had a tale of woe.

Maybe, despite what Rob thought, Kalea Inn *did*

need a dash of Christmas spirit to brighten the mood and hearts of everyone staying there.

CHAPTER FOURTEEN

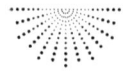

Slowly but surely, Libby was falling in love with Hawaii.

She was used to the fast pace of the marketing world, but here, they did things differently.

It was the most relaxed Christmas she'd ever had. No running to the grocery store a thousand times to stand in mile-long lines. No excessive list of gifts to buy, because Christmas wasn't Christmas if you didn't break your credit card with buying toys and presents.

Then there was the absurd pressure she put on herself to make sure everything was just as her mother and father would have made it when they were alive. The way her siblings expected it.

No, life didn't have to be that way.

Today, the sand was cool as she walked along the

beach in her brand-new swimsuit. She was still a bit bashful so she'd bought a cute floral print, halter neck tankini on her second day on the island. It fit her perfectly and made her feel confident about her body without making her feel exposed.

The wind skated off the ocean sending a cool breeze over her skin. Libby couldn't help but smile at how wonderful it was to feel sand between her toes and smell the salty freshness of the ocean.

She looked out onto the water. Whitecaps peaked the waves, and a lone surfer occupied the water beyond the reef. She stopped to watch.

The waters near the inn weren't the type that called international surfers to try their luck, these were calm and could easily be manoeuvred by a novice.

Beyond the reef, however, the waves were larger, forming into curls, and the surfer was making the most of them. Lowering beneath the barrelling edge of a wave he was a master on the board.

Libby never pretended to be brave. Climbing on a surfboard and going out into water she couldn't stand in and probably couldn't even *swim* in, was not her cup of tea.

However, it didn't mean she didn't appreciate watching those who could. She stood and watched as the surfer tamed the waves and rode the final one into shore not far from where she stood. She stared as he carried his board in, dragging his long dark hair back with a hand before jogging in her direction.

It was only as he got closer that she realized who it was.

Rob nodded at her. "I see you're out early," he commented.

"It's such a beautiful day I thought a walk on the beach would do me good," she answered.

"Just on the beach? The water's perfect."

Libby looked at the ocean. He was right, it did look inviting. "I haven't done much swimming since I got here ..."

"How much have you done?"

"None actually," she laughed. "I've been spending my days wandering or sunbathing or just meeting people. I've met so many nice people since I arrived here. You wouldn't believe some of the stories I've heard."

"I can imagine actually," Rob informed her lightly. "You'd be surprised how many broken-hearted and lonely people end up here."

Libby thought about what he was saying. She'd already encountered several people with stories like those of Naomi, Nate, and Greg.

Even a few like her who felt unappreciated and were seeking a change.

However, she also saw another element. She saw what they were truly after – a getaway from Christmas commercialism to somewhere more laid-back and easygoing, where they could find their own kind of peace and joy away from the noise of traditional festivity.

"Rob, have you ever thought of doing something different for Christmas?" Libby asked then.

His forehead wrinkled. "Like what?"

"Not traditional stuff obviously, but different to what other places offer at this time of year. I'm talking about something beyond the surface. Something that touches the heart."

"I never really thought about it," he admitted as he studied her carefully.

"Well, I have."

Libby took a deep breath. What she was about to suggest was insane and completely none of her business, but it was something that had been nagging her since the other night.

"I work in marketing for a living. I'm used to figuring out what people want and giving it to them. It's how you sell. You give people what they want, or make them *believe* they want something they never even knew they did."

"You think this place needs better marketing?" Rob questioned with some scepticism.

"Not marketing per se. I'm talking about doing something for the people here who are trying to get back to what Christmas is truly about."

The moment the words left her mouth Rob's expression changed. The lines in his forehead smoothed out and he sort of squinted at her.

Then he laughed softly. "That sounds like something Kalea would've said."

Libby wasn't sure if resembling something his late wife would've thought of was good or bad, but it didn't stop her from presenting her case.

"Your wife wanted this place to mean something. You said so yourself. It was her dream. So this year, why don't you make it the dream of all the staff and guests too?"

Rob stuck his board in the sand. "What exactly do you have in mind?"

She smiled. "A day of honouring what Christmas is really all about. No gifts, or spending money on each other; just sharing time together instead."

Rob's small laugh grew to a chuckle as she continued. "You sound more and more like her the more I listen to you."

"Then your wife was a very wise woman," Libby grinned.

Rob's eyes met hers. "She was."

She felt her stomach knot as he looked at her.

"Do you surf?" he asked unexpectedly.

"No," Libby laughed. "I've never even tried."

"I can teach you."

She shook her head. "I don't know about that…"

"I'll make you a deal," he countered. "If you let me teach you the basics about surfing, I'll allow you to execute this … plan of yours."

Libby's eyes grew wide. Did he just say he'd let her run with her idea? She couldn't describe the feeling in her stomach. It was like getting another shot at the promotion she'd missed out on.

"Great. So where do we start?"

"First things first," Rob chuckled. "Hold your board with two hands when you're carrying it out. You can tuck it under your arm like this when you're on the beach," he said as he showed her what to do, then handed the board to her for her to try.

Libby tucked the board under her arm.

"This is going to be too long for you given your height and weight," he informed. "You'd need one more than a foot shorter. But I can still show you a few things with it before we hit the water"

Libby nodded until she realized. "Hit the water?"

"Yes," Rob smiled. "You can't surf if you aren't comfortable out there," he said as he turned toward the water. "I need to see how you handle yourself."

Seems she was going to get wet that morning after all.

CHAPTER FIFTEEN

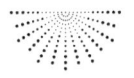

Rob continued to explain the basics of surfing while Libby listened quietly, nodding and following his example when she needed to.

Before she knew it, he was telling her it was time to hit the water. She waded out into the surf as he led the way.

Her heart was beating a bit faster in her chest as the sea climbed higher and higher up along her body.

She was good for a few feet but soon she could no longer feel the bottom and had to begin to tread water.

"You okay?" he asked as he looked back at her. He looked so at home in the ocean. His limbs moved effortlessly to keep him up.

Libby felt like a failed experiment. It had been so

long it felt unnatural. Still, she vaguely remembered what to do.

"Yes. I'm fine," she replied.

He smiled at her and held out his hand. "Take my hand."

Libby didn't think twice about the offer. A second later he'd pulled her to him and they were face-to-face.

"You sure you're okay?"

"Yes," she said a little breathlessly. "I just haven't been swimming in a long time. I just need to get back in the swing of things."

"Don't be scared," he said firmly, but comfortingly. "I've got you."

She nodded as he led her closer to the reef. She wasn't sure how deep the water was, but she knew it was a lot darker beneath than it had been before.

"Do you think you can hold your breath?" Rob asked.

"Why?" she asked with just a pinch of fear.

"There's something I'd like to show you, but you have to go underwater to see it," he said as the waves lapped around his shoulders. He once again raked a hand through his hair to remove it from his face.

"Okay. Show me."

"Hold your breath."

Libby did as she was told, and the next second she was descending beneath the waves. She blinked several times to adjust her eyes to the salt. The moment they did so, the most spectacular sight greeted her.

Waving fans and corals of multiple colours stretched out before her. Some looked like fingers and others looked like spines. More looked like purple flower clusters.

A turtle swam by and Rob turned to point it out as it approached. Above the water it was amazing but below, it was … incredible. The turtle was at least three feet long with a head and fins covered in dark scales.

Libby breathed deeply as her head broke the surface. Rob was still beneath. He was better at holding his breath than she was.

The waves were rolling in faster now. The tide seemed to be coming in.

"What did you think?" he asked when they'd both resurfaced.

"It was spectacular."

"Maybe I can take you snorkelling some time and we can see more of it," he suggested.

"I'd love that. But right now," she said as her head

bobbed above another wave. "I think we should go back. The tide's getting a little higher."

Rob seemed completely unaffected, but Libby was getting nervous.

They swam back side-by-side and sat on the shore after, enjoying the sun. It warmed her skin and Libby couldn't remember having a better time in her life.

Rob turned to her. "So what do you need me to do for this Christmas plan of yours?" he asked.

Libby smiled. "Not much. I think I've got this covered."

CHAPTER SIXTEEN

It was quite shocking to Libby how many people were just skating through the holidays, hoping to stay above water.

Some wanted to forget. Some needed money. Others, like her, just wanted to escape Christmas.

The more people she talked to, the more Libby realized the idea was a lot bigger than she imagined.

One example was Tua, one of the waiters from the dining room. He had no family and saw the holidays as a time to distract himself from the fact that he was alone.

Ululani, one of the girls who cleaned the rooms, had a family that had fallen on hard times. Her mother and father were both out of work and she had six younger siblings to take care of. She was nineteen and the sole breadwinner. She was working because if she didn't they'd have nothing to even remotely resemble the Christmases they once enjoyed.

Though Libby wasn't just learning the bad, but the good too.

"Every year my mother would make these amazing coconut biscuits," Ululani said with a smile. "They were like dog biscuits almost, really hard with a good crack and so much flavour. We'd help her roll them out, cut them up and then bake them."

"What about this year?" Libby questioned.

Ulalani shook her head. "Not this year."

"Why not?' she asked. "You can still hold on to the good despite everything."

"Tell that to my mother," Ululani answered. "Since she and Dad lost their jobs they've sort of lost themselves as well. They worry and they try to find work. That's all they do. Now it's Christmas and nothing is the same. This is the third holiday since it happened. The first year they tried, believing that work would come. The second, things weren't so great. This year is horrible. If it weren't for Rob letting me work here, I don't know what we'd do."

"He seems like a really good guy," Libby stated.

"The best," Ululani said as she turned the sheet

over at the top and tucked it beneath the mattress. "It's a shame he's always alone."

"What do you mean?"

"You know. He doesn't have anyone. You'd think someone like him would be drowning in women, but he barely even notices them," the young woman divulged.

"Seriously?"

"Yeah. I guess he still misses his wife."

"Did you know her?"

"No. She died before I found out about this place, but Honi who works in maintenance, he was here from the very beginning. He said she was a great woman. Kind, like Rob and that everyone was really sorry when she died." She sighed. "They said if he hadn't had this place to hold onto, they weren't sure he would've made it."

Libby considered what Ululani was saying.

It seemed that the person with the most need for a change in their perspective was Rob.

"Ululani, I'll see you later," she said as she got to her feet and headed for the door.

"Okay, see you, Libby," the young woman replied as she continued to work on her bed.

She went to the office to look for Rob but he

wasn't there. She checked the rest of the inn and he wasn't there either.

"Can I help with anything?" a staff member asked as she entered the kitchen.

"I was looking for Rob."

"Oh he's at home," the woman replied. "He's got a house just up the beach."

"Thanks," Libby said in a rush as she turned and left. She stopped short. "Which direction?"

"North."

She might be overstepping calling on Rob like this, but she needed to tell him what she was thinking.

Christmas was just a few days away and if they wanted to do this properly, they had to do it now.

CHAPTER SEVENTEEN

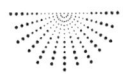

The walk was longer than she thought, but soon a Tiffany blue-colored beach house with white trim came into view.

Libby stood on the sand looking at it.

There was a gate that led in from the beach to a small yard area and she wondered if she should just walk in, or if she should call out to Rob first and let him know she was there.

In the end, the choice wasn't hers to make; he saw her before she had a chance to do anything.

"Libby? What are you doing here?" he asked as he looked at her over the line of fresh laundry. He was shirtless and his hair was pulled back in a low ponytail.

"I came to talk to you."

"Come on in," he said casually as he continued to hang out his laundry.

She let herself in by the gate and came to stand beside him. "Want some help?"

"Sure." He tossed a damp pillowcase at her and smiled. "You can talk while you help me hang these out."

Libby began pinning laundry to the line.

"So I think I've finalized my idea for a different kind of Christmas."

"Oh?" Rob asked as he grabbed a pair of pants from the basket and hung them next to the sheet.

"We need to remember and honour the good. Bad things happen, but good things do too. We need to focus on that. We can each do something that reminds us of the special times we had, at Christmas and otherwise."

Rob stopped what he was doing and turned to look at her. A smile began to spread across his face.

"Kalea used to do this thing … what the Hawaiian people used to do before they celebrated Thanksgiving as we know it, and it happened on the last day of December."

She smiled. "So why don't we do something like that? A day of remembering the best things about our lives. A day to forget all the bad?"

He stared at her, his eyes wandering along her face as if he were looking for something.

"You don't like the idea?" she questioned finally when he remained quiet.

"No," he said calmly. "I do. It's just … it really is the kind of thing Kalea would've loved."

"Rob," Libby said as her hands picked up another pillowcase and held it. "I don't know anything about your wife. I don't know what it must've been like to lose someone you loved that much, but I do know that no one who loved you would ever want you to go through life hurting because of them."

The words stunned even herself as they left her lips. They sunk in as though they were a warning to her too.

She'd been trying to live up to the standards her parents had set instead of making her own. Each year for the holidays she was trying to replicate something that was her mother's and what was expected, instead of doing her own thing.

He laughed softly. "That also sounds like something she'd say."

"Then listen," Libby continued. "Do something that's going to remind you that your wife really loved this time of year. That it meant something to her because of the love she could share and the lives she could touch. You may have lost her physically, but the spirit of what she believed in isn't gone. It's still in you. You kept the inn open in her name. So now run it the way she would want you to. Touch the lives she knew you could."

"What makes you think she believed I could touch lives?" Rob questioned.

"I know that every one of your employees thinks you're amazing. The people you allow to come here, all think highly of you and have good things to say, even if they do think you're a little aloof."

"Aloof? Who said I was aloof?"

"I did," Libby admitted. "I wondered why you were kind of distant. If you were just a big old grump or if there was something more. Then I got to know you and I realized you weren't grumpy. You were just lonely."

"You got that?" he asked as he took a step toward her.

"Yes, I did. The thing is, with loneliness, there's a sure-fire cure."

"What's that?"

"Surround yourself with people and things that make you forget it. That's what I want to do for you and everyone at the inn. I want this Christmas to be a day when we can all forget our troubles and embrace all the good there still is to this life."

He nodded. "Then let's do it. What do you need?"

"First, we need to include all the guests, staff and their families. We can invite them to do the things they love most. Bake their favourite pies or write down their fondest stories or memories to share. Also, why don't we decorate? Not too much, but a festive appearance really does lift the mood and add some cheer. We could ask everyone to pitch in and use *their* favourite decorations. Popcorn garlands, tinsel, lights, whatever reminds them of the best time of their lives even if it isn't necessarily what you might think of as Christmas."

"Libby, I hope they pay you well at your job because you have some pretty good ideas," Rob commented and she blushed.

"Actually, I lost out on a big promotion right before I came here," she admitted.

"You did mention something about that the night we were talking with Nate and Greg."

"Ah, I'm sure I'll get another chance sometime in the future," she replied as she turned from him to hang out the other pillowcase.

It still burned to speak about the disappointment,

but she knew that it was something she was going to have to get over.

"Libby?" Rob called as he laid a hand over hers. She stopped what she was doing. "Yes?"

"Don't you think you maybe need to take some of this advice too?" he said in a low voice.

"I know," she admitted hesitantly.

"So why don't we make another deal?" Rob suggested as he removed his hand from hers and she turned to look at him. "I'll let you turn my entire business upside down - do all you've suggested if you'll throw yourself completely into this plan. I want one hundred per cent. Nothing holding you back. No memories of what might have been. If I have to do it then you do too. Agreed?"

She looked at him as a slight embarrassment coloured her cheeks. "Agreed."

CHAPTER EIGHTEEN

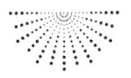

Rob walked her back to the inn afterwards. The walk wasn't nearly as long as it was when she'd set out to reach him.

It seemed to go by far too quickly as they talked.

The first person they met was Naomi. She was walking on the beach collecting shells. It was a pastime she and her husband had enjoyed together.

"Hello, you two? Taking a stroll?" she called out as she spotted them approach.

"Just heading back," Libby said with a smile.

"We were planning something we think you'd enjoy, Naomi," Rob commented. "A day to celebrate."

"Oh?"

"Instead of just Christmas, we want to look at the things that make it really special for each of us and share those things with others," Libby explained. "A day to embrace only the good and forget all the bad."

Naomi looked at her thoughtfully, then a smile began to spread across her face. "I think that's a wonderful idea. In this world, we spend far too much time worrying about the negative. My Charlie never did. He always looked at the grass being greener."

"Then you'll participate?" Libby asked enthusiastically. She was eager to see this idea through in reality, and if they could get everyone to jump on board the better it would be.

"I will definitely," Naomi asserted. "I'll see if I can't get some of the others to join us too."

"Do that," Rob answered. "We want staff and guests to come. I plan to announce it tonight at dinner."

"You should probably get some fliers printed …" Naomi suggested.

"I can do that in my office, but I need someone to design them," Rob said.

"I can design them if you have Adobe or some other software," Libby suggested.

"I'm sure I've got something you can use."

"Then you figure out what to say and I'll work on getting the fliers made." Libby could feel the excitement building. It almost felt like the day of the

Hershell presentation, but far less stressful and a lot more fun.

"You two sound like a good team," Naomi commented, silencing them both.

"Libby's very talented," Rob said. "She makes things easier."

"Don't mind Rob," Libby said with a chuckle. "He just likes to make his guests feel good about themselves."

"I'd say he's speaking the truth," Naomi agreed.

She could feel her cheeks getting hot. Praise wasn't something Libby was used to, nor something she hardly considered, but the sincerity with which Rob was speaking also made her feel something more.

CHAPTER NINETEEN

Christmas Eve came faster than Libby expected and the atmosphere around the inn had completely changed.

Home-made garlands and wreaths hung around the building. The staff were smiling and so were the guests as they helped in the decorating project. Everyone contributed something, whether it was a garland, a food dish or a story.

Every guest also had something to do, and Libby was completely submerged in this lovely new alternative approach to Christmas.

Naomi was spearheading activities in the kitchen, along with the cook. Two other guests were there making some of their family Christmas favorites, while Ululani was making the dough for her mother's cookies.

Her entire family was invited, as well as several other family members of the staff.

"Naomi, everything smells fantastic," Libby commented as she entered the kitchen to see how things were rounding out. The event was starting in an hour.

"Thank you," she said with a smile, "but it isn't all me. The girls have worked so well together."

The cook laughed as did the other women. "We make a good team," the cook replied.

Most of the food was made by her, but a lot of the dishes were suggested by the guests who knew what they wanted but weren't as skilled at cooking as others.

Everyone was finding their place in this crazy plan and Libby believed it was going to turn out fantastic.

Once she'd checked in with the kitchen and made sure that the music and everything else was ready, she headed to her room to get dressed.

Rob had been a surprise too. He'd really come around to her idea and had ended up being the one leading the decorating.

Now, he was climbing on top of the building with a Santa and Mrs Claus in shorts and floral print shirts and reindeer with leis around their necks. It looked fun and spectacular all at once.

Libby's dress was bright red and she'd bought a pair of kitten heels for the evening. Her brown hair was swept up in a messy twist and she'd even bothered to do her makeup.

If she was honest, it was the most excited she'd felt about Christmas in years.

SHE MET Rob again on the stairs as she was making her way down to the dining room. She smiled and gave him a small wave as she ascended.

"You look great," he said as he assessed her outfit. He was wearing dark blue jeans and a white ribbed shirt. His hair was down and slicked back.

"So do you," she replied as he held out his arm for her to take it. "Shall we head to the dining room?"

"We shall," Libby answered with a grin, mimicking his formal tone, and the pair began to walk together.

"How are you feeling about this evening?" he asked as they meandered through the lobby. Libby wasn't sure but it almost felt as if Rob was prolonging their arrival.

"Honestly, I'm a bit nervous," she admitted. "I really

want this to work and for everyone to have a good time."

"Don't worry. They will," he assured her. "It was a great idea."

"Thanks. I couldn't have done anything in the first place if you hadn't consented to my hare-brained scheme."

"And I wouldn't be feeling this good if I didn't either."

Libby's face stilled and her heart quickened. "Do you mean that?

He nodded. "I'd forgotten how great this time of year used to be. You reminded me of that. I don't think I can thank you enough."

She blushed. 'Don't mention it. It was my pleasure. And you know, I think I needed this too."

CHAPTER TWENTY

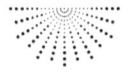

They walked into the dining room to find everyone already gathered together.

Rob left Libby to take his place as MC at the top of the room. He grabbed the microphone already set up with the sound system and got the festivities started.

"Good evening ladies and gentlemen. Guests, staff and family, I'd like to welcome you to the Kalea Inn's holiday celebration. This evening is a time to remember all the good things we've experienced in our lives and for one day put aside the unpleasant stuff. I know you must be thinking, 'Why?' and the answer is simple really. Why not?"

A soft murmur of laughter rippled across the room.

"Many of us tend to get so caught up in the

commercial aspects of Christmas, we overlook the true meaning of the holidays. My late wife used to so love this time of year," he admitted as the room fell silent. "I lost her on Christmas Eve six years ago. I didn't think I'd ever have a happy Christmas again - until now."

Libby stood rapt, listening to Rob pour his heart out. She marvelled at the way he was able to open up when he'd seemed so closed off when she arrived.

"Then someone reminded me that we need to remember the good. We need to think about the things we tend to forget once we allow the bad stuff to overwhelm us. The bad memories. The misfortunes. The losses. Today, they don't exist. Today we are celebrating only the good."

Libby smiled again as Rob turned to look at her.

"Now I'd like to thank the person who came up with this idea. The person who helped me remember what this time of year truly means. You all know her. She's the one who's been running around making sure you all took part today," he mused. "Libby, thank you - for being you. For being the kind of person who cares about others and who cares enough about all of us here to bring this idea to life. You brought the festive back to this place and all of us. Thank you."

Libby's face was red, she knew it. She hadn't expected him to single her out.

Applause filled the room and several encouraging hands touched her shoulder to confirm their agreement with Rob's comments. She didn't know what to say.

Then he passed the mic to the person to his right, and the chorus of thanks and remembrance began.

Everyone sat listening once things got started. People shared their best childhood memories. Some were of Christmas, others of the people they loved.

Naomi shared her most cherished memories with her husband and the funny thing he'd do every Christmas Day. Charlie sounded like an incredible man, and Naomi was smiling with every word she spoke.

That was exactly what Libby wanted. For people to remember only the good.

Greg stood when it was his turn. He looked fondly at his older brother. "The great thing I remember most about my life, other than Mom, is my brother, right here," he said as he held out his hand to Nate. "Typically, we honour people when it's too late to tell them how we feel about them. I don't want to do that. I want my brother to know how much he means to me right now, while he's here, and why I'm glad that he's my brother. I couldn't ask for a better sibling. You have always been there to guide me and help me and I'm glad that I can be there for you now. I love you."

Everyone smiled and applauded as the two brothers embraced. Libby dabbed the corner of her eyes as she listened. This was more than she'd expected, but everything she'd hoped for too.

CHAPTER TWENTY-ONE

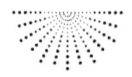

"Finally, the last person to share something this evening. Libby," Rob said, as he handed her the mic.

She was trembling as she took it.

"Thank you," she replied and the mic made a piercing noise. She squinted her eyes as it stung her ears. A moment later the problem was settled. "Thank you," she repeated. "The best times I ever had were with my late parents. They were two of the most loving and committed people I've ever met. They were the glue that held our family together, and I wanted to be just like my mother when I got older. She was the one who made it all work. She was the one who could read us all like a book and solve our problems even before we asked."

"She must've been related to mine," Nate commented and everyone chuckled.

"Maybe," Libby answered. "She seemed to be related to everyone," she mused. "Everyone certainly loved her like she was an aunt or a sister."

Libby was standing in the room, but her mind was somewhere else as she continued.

"Theirs was the love that inspired the kind of love I wanted to have in my life. They set the standard I've aspired to ever since. If it wasn't going to be a love like theirs then I didn't want it. I didn't want to settle for second best or second place. I wanted a love that made you want to be with that person no matter where they went. And while I still might be waiting for that," Libby continued with an ironic chuckle. "I know that it's out there. Real love, the kind that lasts, does exist, and it waits for the right time to make an appearance, but when it does, you'll never forget it."

Applause once again filled the room as she finished her little speech. Her heart was racing in her chest but at least she'd gotten through it. It was amazing. She did presentations for a living but the nervousness never went away, no matter how many times she stood before a crowd to speak.

Once the more personal element was over, it was

time for the music and the food. People left their tables and lined up at the buffet to sample the best of Hawaiian cuisine and the mishmash of other favourite personal festive recipes the guests and staff had come up with.

"Libby," Rob called as he pulled her aside. "I just wanted to say thank you again."

"You don't need to," she answered. "You're making too big a deal out of this."

"I don't think so." He gestured around the room. "Look at this. Look at everyone's faces. This is thanks to you. No one else could've done it," he commented.

"She has that effect on people," a familiar voice agreed from behind her. "She always has. Ever since she was a kid."

Libby turned in surprise to find that the words had been spoken by none other than her brother.

CHAPTER TWENTY-TWO

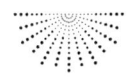

She couldn't believe her eyes. There of all people was Andy, backpack slung over his arm and a smile on his face.

"What on earth are you doing here?" she asked in surprise.

"I came to get you," he replied jauntily.

Libby turned to Rob, who was looking from her brother to her and back again.

"It's alright," he murmured, his voice cold once again. "I'll give you two a moment."

"Wait," she called out. "You don't have to go. My brother was just leaving."

She watched as Rob's expression changed. "Your brother?"

"Yes. Andy, this is Rob."

Andy duly took the hand Rob offered in greeting. Libby wasn't happy to see him though.

This was her trip, her escape and he was ruining it by being there. Then, to make matters worse, she saw her sister appear in the doorway. "You brought Eden too?" she asked in disbelief.

"I knew I was going to need reinforcements to get you to come home," he replied. "So brought the best."

"But how did you guys even know where I was?" Libby questioned.

"I think the three of you need to talk. You can use my office," Rob offered, as he pulled the keys from his pocket and handed them to Libby. He stepped closer and whispered in her ear. "Face your problems. Don't run from them."

She looked at him pleadingly, but she knew it was no use. He was right and her siblings had come all this way after all. "Follow me."

Libby led them to Rob's office. She flicked on the light as they entered before she stood in the middle of the room, her arms folded over her chest,

"See that," Eden said as she walked in. "We're in trouble. She's doing the folded arm thing like Mom used to."

"What do you two want?"

"Libs, it's Christmas. A time of family and togetherness, like Mom and Dad always wanted," Andy answered.

"It isn't the same without you," Eden added.

"Why? Because there's no one to get the house ready, cook all the food, clean up after and do your shopping and childminding?" Libby chided. "That's not what Mom and Dad would want, and neither do I."

"We know. We were wrong," Andy said. "We took you for granted and we're sorry for that. It's just … you always get it done. Everything always comes easier to you and I don't know, I guess we never considered that you'd need help too."

"I worked my butt off on that Hershell project and you took my laptop to New York. I lost my big shot and you acted like it was nothing. A melted candy bar to be replaced. It was my dream and you didn't even care."

"I'm a terrible brother," Andy agreed. "I know that. You disappearing like that really made me realise it."

"Made us all realise it," Eden confirmed. "We understood how much we took you for granted, and how much our lives weren't the same without you being there, and not because you do so much for us, but because you're the sunshine at this time of year, Libby. You're the one who makes it so we don't miss Mom and Dad as much because we know you've got it all covered by focusing on the good stuff, just the way they'd like."

"But I can't do that anymore," she replied. "I can't do it the way they would want, or what you would want. I need to do it the way I know best and not try to be anyone else. I also need you guys to play a part. You leave me with everything like I'm a servant, and when you call you just expect me to drop what I'm doing and help you. I know it's my fault for that in a way too. I let you get away with it in the first place, but now I'm not. I've asked for help. I've begged for help. Now, I'm doing what I feel like."

"And you should," Eden said, to Libby's surprise. "You deserve to have the kind of Christmas you want, with the people you want to share it with. I see everything you've done here. When we arrived everyone was talking about this being your idea and they were so excited about it."

"If this is where you'd rather be, then we'll head back home on the first flight tomorrow without you, but if you want to come home, then we've already booked you a flight back. It's all paid for," Andy confirmed.

Libby was about to answer when something stopped her. What *did* she want? Wasn't it this, what was happening right now - for her family to appreciate her?

She might have helped bring joy to Kalea Inn, but the best thing for her right now was making things right with her family.

Greg was right. Family needed to show how much they cared for each other now, not later. It was what her parents would have wanted too, and Libby had to admit she missed her siblings. Not speaking to them wasn't natural, especially at this time of year.

She sighed. "Already paid for?"

"Yes," Andy said with a smile as he glanced at Eden. "Does that mean you'll come home?"

Libby sighed. "It isn't Christmas without you all either," she admitted. "Despite my desire to escape you guys, being away only made me miss you all the more."

"We missed you too," Eden said as she stepped forward and hugged her tightly.

"I'm sorry little sis," said Andy, joining in. "And I promise we'll make this right. I swear."

CHAPTER TWENTY-THREE

"You're all set," the receptionist said cheerily when Libby checked out out the following morning.

Her flight was leaving in two hours and she, Andy and Eden were headed to the airport.

"Is Rob around?" Libby asked. She hadn't seen him since the night before when she informed him that she would be cutting her trip short to go home and spend Christmas with her family.

He'd seemed happy about it, but Libby sensed he was a little disappointed in her too. She'd done so much to help him out and then she was leaving just as things had gotten better.

"He hasn't been in yet today," the young woman replied. "Sorry to hear you're leaving us so soon. Last night was so amazing. Everyone thought so. I wonder if the tradition will continue next Christmas once you're gone?"

"I'm sure it will," Libby asserted. "I'm sure Rob will see to that." She wasn't sure if she meant it, or if she was just trying to convince herself.

She wasn't sure how it happened, but she'd come to really care about all the people she'd met at Kalea Inn, especially its owner. She'd hate to think that Rob would allow what just happened here; all the beautiful memories and companionship the guests had shared, to fade and for him to fall back into his cloud of melancholy and loneliness.

"Did you want to leave a message for him? I can pass it on when he gets in."

Libby hesitated and then asked for a piece of paper and a pen.

She folded the note and wrote Rob's name on the front.

"Libs, we need to go, the taxi is here," Eden called from the doorway.

"I'm coming," she replied as she walked toward the exit. Then turned back to look at the inn once more.

In a short time, it had made such a big impact on her life. She'd miss it, but maybe sometime in the future, she could return.

"Libby," a voice called out then.

"Hey," she smiled broadly, as the older woman walked toward her. Naomi reached up with her frail arms and gave Libby a hug.

"I heard you were leaving," she said. "Take care of yourself OK. Don't forget us."

"I could never forget you," Libby answered as she hugged her again. "I promise, when I get back home I'll give you a call, just to see how you're doing."

Naomi smiled. "I'd like that."

"Libby," her sister called again.

"I have to go," She gave Naomi one final smile. "It was really nice meeting you."

"It was really nice meeting you too. Merry Christmas."

Libby couldn't stop thinking about this trip as the taxi drove them to the airport.

Nothing had turned out the way she thought, but at the same time, it had been infinitely better.

Her only regret was she and Rob not being able to say goodbye. It felt wrong somehow, after everything.

But she thought sadly, there was nothing she could do about that now.

CHAPTER TWENTY-FOUR

They arrived at the airport on time and Andy took care of checking in their bags.

"Just a few more minutes and we'll be on our way," Eden mused. "Megan is so happy you decided to come home. She's doing her best to make sure you get a proper Pearson family Christmas when you get there."

Libby's eyes widened. "I hope someone hired a caterer."

"She did actually."

They were still laughing together when a familiar voice called her name.

"Hey," Rob greeted softly, as he got close.

Libby colored, despite herself. "I was hoping I'd get to see you before I left."

Her sister smiled and duly stepped away.

"Well, I wasn't sure if I should say goodbye, but when I got your note I knew I had to." He stepped closer and touched her arm. "I couldn't let you go without saying what's been on my mind …. or in my heart."

Libby looked at him in surprise, and her heart beat louder in her ears.

"Before you came along, I was sleep-walking through the remainder of my life hoping to never wake up, but you did. You woke me up. You made me feel again. You reminded me of all the good that life still has to offer if we just hold on to it. So that's why I'm here. I'm trying to hold on to some of the good, Libby. You."

Her eyes widened in surprise. "Rob, what are you saying?"

"I'm saying I can't lose this chance. I've been dead inside for so long, and you made me feel alive again. You've made me remember how to feel good about Christmas. I can't let you go back home without letting you know that I care about you. And that I want to see more of you."

"Rob…" She tried to interrupt but he was unburdening his heart and he wouldn't be stopped.

"I know it's crazy. We live so far apart and long-distance relationships are tough, but if you're willing to give it a shot, I am too."

An instant smile turned up the corners of Libby's mouth as his words settled in her heart. "Do you mean that?"

"Every word," he answered with a smile of his own. "I know you've decided to go home for Christmas, but if I suggested I maybe come visit you for New Year, would you object?"

She laughed in disbelief. "I wouldn't object," Libby said, still laughing nervously as he stepped closer. "I'd be delighted."

"Do you know you have the best smile….when I see it I can't help but stare at you."

"Is that all?" she asked boldly.

"Actually, it makes me want to kiss you," he continued with a grin. "I just wonder if you'd let me."

"Is that a question?"

"More like a consideration," Rob murmured then softly lowered his lips to hers.

They met somewhere in between. A place between Minnesota and Hawaii, and heaven and earth.

Libby certainly felt as if she were flying as Rob pulled her into his strong arms and held her there.

She was giddy by the time they parted.

An announcement rang over the loudspeaker. Her flight was being called.

"That's me," she chuckled regretfully.

"I'll let you know when I've got all my plans settled," Rob said, as he forced himself to release her.

"If you change your mind, don't tell me OK? It'll be easier that way."

"I'll be there," he said confidently. "You have my word."

She stepped up and kissed him again, a quick one this time as she rushed to meet the others and board the flight.

A FEW MINUTES LATER, Libby was seated and looking out the window of the aircraft as she waited for it to take off.

Christmas had taken on an entirely new meaning for her now. She'd discovered a new way of doing things and found someone whose heart understood hers.

Better yet, his was leading him to Minnesota for New Year's.

The engines hummed to life and she felt excitement build up inside her.

The plane was about to take off, but Libby's heart

already had. Her life was changing, she could feel it. And it was all for the better.

All because of her wonderful Christmas escape.

Hope you enjoyed this THE CHRISTMAS ESCAPE. Read on for an excerpt of another Melissa Hill festive story, THE HOLIDAY SWAP - now airing as a Christmas movie!

THE HOLIDAY SWAP

EXCERPT

CHAPTER ONE

It was unbelievable how a couple of snow flurries could make everyone in Boston suddenly forget how to drive, Ally Walker mused, frustrated as she sat in the back of the taxi winging its way to the airport.

Granted, it wasn't often they made it all the way till December without any significant accumulations. But none of that especially mattered right now. All she could think about was making her flight.

"Outta the way!" her cab driver remonstrated as the car in front stopped suddenly at the airport terminal's no-stopping zone.

Ally scooted towards the edge of the back seat in an attempt to see out of the windshield. "You know what ... this is good. I can walk the rest of the way."

The driver pulled up to the curb, and tapping her

phone to pay him, (adding a nice holiday tip) she exited the car quickly and hopped round back to grab her stuff from the trunk. Extending the pull handle of her carry-on suitcase, she was off and running into the terminal building, not even letting her three-inch pumps slow her down.

Using her free hand to pull her trench coat tighter around her body and her wool sheath dress, Ally attempted to create a barrier against the bitter cold. And questioned what she could have been thinking this morning not wearing pantyhose while bitter snow flurries pelted her bare legs.

Inside, she made it to the security line in quick time. After years of practice, Ally could do this in her sleep. Which was fortunate because after a non-stop work day that began at 5 am this morning, she *felt* half asleep.

"Come on, come on," she muttered impatiently as she waited for the airline app to load so she could pull up her digital boarding pass.

But with 'no reservation found' displaying onscreen, Ally reluctantly gave up her place in the line to call her assistant.

"Walters Tech," Mel answered, in her most professional and chipper voice.

"It's me," Ally greeted, trying not to make herself

sound too demanding, but time was of the essence. "Why can't I check-in for my flight?"

"You know you're not with your usual, right? They don't fly into your friend's location. I thought I'd mentioned that. "

Ally winced. She hated changes of plan.

"I didn't know that. Text me the info? Maybe if I run to the gate I can still make it."

"Yeah you're cutting it kinda close, considering…"

"I had to make a stop by my apartment on the way," Ally explained, glancing at the garment bag laid carefully on top of her luggage, sequins sparkling brightly through the plastic covering.

She'd fallen instantly in love with the dress nearly four years ago when she happened to pass by it in a department store window and threw caution to the wind, purchasing it without any particular occasion in mind.

Since then the gown had been sitting in her closet, just waiting for the right moment to shine. And in her suitcase was a gorgeous pair of silver heels with jewelled straps she'd purchased a week later to match.

Just in case an opportunity presented itself, which it seemed would happen this weekend, courtesy of Ally's best friend Lara's invite to the Snow Ball, a gala event being held in her Maine hometown.

A girl couldn't just wear any old shoes with *that* dress.

Ally hadn't put much else thought into packing for this particular visit though, since her friend had more clothes than Saks and she and Lara were pretty much the same size.

Lara's was by all accounts a *very* small town, so she figured most other outings while there would call for a pretty casual dress code.

Besides, the visit was just a short festive diversion from her final destination; Florida, which called for shorts, bikinis and not a whole lot else.

Ally always preferred to travel light.

"You wouldn't *believe* how crowded the airport is today," she muttered to Mel now.

Ally had flown over 100,000 miles that year and never had to fight her way through this many people. All of them just taking their time, walking in large groups, talking, laughing, carrying huge wrapped gifts.

Didn't they know about gift cards? Or online shopping? Granted she had a couple of small things in her luggage for Lara's kids, but they barely took up any room.

Ally prided herself on travelling light.

"Two days before Christmas and you didn't expect it to be crowded?" her assistant laughed.

"Well, Christmas Eve and Day are usually quiet; that's why they're usually my favourite days to fly," she said, scowling at a man who'd almost rolled his suitcase right over her toes.

"Because most people spend those days with family, not travelling on vacation," Mel said. "Which reminds me, you're all set for your usual Clearwater Beach hotel. As soon as Christmas is done, you'll be en route to palm trees and sunshine."

Which to Ally right about now, sounded like heaven.

CHAPTER TWO

She certainly wouldn't be getting any sunshine and palm trees in upstate Maine.

Looking around again at the crammed airport, Ally started to doubt whether she'd made the right decision to visit Lara and her family for the holidays, rather than going straight to Florida.

But time spent with her old friend was long overdue and since she hadn't yet visited her friend's house, and rarely took time off from her tech consulting business, this time of year was a good opportunity as any.

"Thanks, Mel," she said to her assistant now. "Enjoy your time off, and Merry Christmas."

Out of breath a little from running in heels, Ally

scrambled to check in at the other airline's digital kiosk with only minutes to spare.

As her boarding pass printed, a sudden horror filled her when she saw the seat number printed next to her name. Not only was this the first time in recent memory she hadn't been upgraded, but to add insult to injury, they had the nerve to ask her to board in the *final* group.

Ally had been pretty much royalty on the biggest airline in the country for the last four years in a row thanks to her weekly travel schedule and copious air miles.

SkyAir rewarded her for her loyalty by treating her like gold. She was usually the first one on the aircraft, whereupon she almost always enjoyed a complimentary upgrade to first or business class.

What would it be like to fly as a regular person again?

She barely had time to think about what lay ahead as she hurried onwards to her gate.

"Last call, boarding group #5," someone called over the loudspeaker just as she arrived. Looking around the gate, Ally saw only four other people waiting to board.

She quickly scanned her pass and wheeled her bag

through, only to find the line at a standstill on the jet bridge.

No doubt the passengers already onboard were searching for overhead space or playing musical chairs with their fellow seatmates trying to secure seats next to the family members they were travelling with.

As if it would be so difficult to spend a two-hour flight apart.

"Ma'am," a flight attendant approached her then. "I'm afraid we are going to have to check your luggage today."

"Excuse me?" Ally asked, in the hope she'd misheard. Her bag was TSA-approved. It fit perfectly in the overhead storage compartment and was just the right size to hold her clothing, her work computer and toiletries. This lady had to be mistaken.

"Overhead storage is limited on these smaller puddle hoppers," she explained pleasantly. "Don't worry, we'll just store it beneath the hold and it will be waiting for you at the carousel on the other side."

Worry wasn't the right word. Annoyed was more like it. Though not wanting to prolong the boarding process any further, Ally reluctantly handed over her case, first grabbing her garment bag off the top.

"OK, well is there somewhere on board I could hang this maybe?" she asked.

"We only have a small area for the crew's items. We're not supposed to, but that dress is gorgeous. It would be a real shame if it got wrinkled."

"Thank you," Ally smiled gratefully, as the attendant took the garment bag and headed back out the gate.

A little bit of separation anxiety kicked in and she felt compelled to watch as her trusty suitcase and favourite dress were spirited away somewhere.

It occurred to Ally then she hadn't arranged for a bag tag, but before she had time to get the flight attendant's attention, the line started moving again and she needed to keep up.

Ally attempted one final peek behind when the line once again stopped abruptly and she collided with a taller man in front. His plaid sports coat felt soft again on her cheek and she was close enough to see the slight wear in the leather patches at the elbows.

Assuming he was older based on his style of clothing, when he turned around she was surprised to find that he was in fact, much younger - likely in his early thirties, just like her.

And cute.

"Pardon me," he apologised gently, his blue eyes laser-focused on hers and normally, the intensity of such a gaze would make Ally uncomfortable.

But this gave her time to study his face. She could see that his eyes also had specks of green, his nose was straight and his square jawline was covered with light stubble. He looked like the kind of guy who would normally be clean shaven, but for some reason had skipped his morning shave for a day or two.

"No, my fault," she mumbled. "I wasn't paying attention."

Ally was almost sorry when he broke their eye contact as the line began to move again, leaving her to stare at the back of his head once more.

Maybe boarding last wasn't so bad after all.

END OF EXCERPT.

THE HOLIDAY SWAP is out now in print and ebook.

Printed in Great Britain
by Amazon

39470657R00078